NL

 **W9-AMO-172**

12/2021

THE SNOOPY SHOW

WHEN SNOOPY MET WOODSTOCK

by Charles M. Schulz

Based on *The Snoopy Show* episode "When Snoopy Met Woodstock"

written by Laurie Elliott

Adapted by Ximena Hastings

Ready-to-Read

Simon Spotlight

New York   London   Toronto   Sydney   New Delhi

SIMON SPOTLIGHT
An imprint of Simon & Schuster Children's Publishing Division
1230 Avenue of the Americas, New York, NY 10020
This Simon Spotlight edition August 2021
Peanuts and all related titles, logos, and characters are trademarks of Peanuts
Worldwide LLC © 2021 Peanuts Worldwide LLC.
Manufactured in the United States of America 0721 LAK
10 9 8 7 6 5 4 3 2 1
ISBN 978-1-5344-8557-0 (hc)
ISBN 978-1-5344-8556-3 (pbk)
ISBN 978-1-5344-8558-7 (ebook)

Snoopy and Woodstock are
playing football together.

They are the best of friends!

But they weren't always friends. . . .

Woodstock used to fly
with a flock of birds.

They loved to fly together,
but Woodstock had a hard
time keeping up.

One day, Woodstock got tired and fell from the sky onto . . .

Shocked, Snoopy nudged
Woodstock off his doghouse. He
put on his aviator hat and goggles.

Woodstock didn't mind, though. He hopped right back on. He wanted to learn to be a pilot, just like Snoopy!

Snoopy stomped away.
He was the only pilot
of his doghouse!

Snoopy decided to go fishing.
Nothing was more relaxing.
He reeled in his fishing line and
pulled out . . . Woodstock!

Snoopy tossed Woodstock back
into the water and decided to play
a card game alone.

But with every move, Woodstock
was there, chirping suggestions
loudly.

When it was lunchtime, Snoopy went to the park for a picnic.

As Snoopy was enjoying a nap, Woodstock flew out of the picnic basket!

Snoopy was very annoyed.
He went to see Lucy at her
psychiatric booth.

He told Lucy that Woodstock was
following him around everywhere!

"Are you almost done?"
Lucy complained. "I have another
appointment with a yellow bird
who just wants to be friends with
a dog!"

Snoopy was surprised.
Woodstock wanted to be his . . .
friend?

Snoopy went back to his doghouse
and made himself a snack.

Right before he took a sip of his
root beer, he spotted a yellow tail.

Suddenly, Woodstock hopped out
of the glass. He was covered in
foam and bubbles! Snoopy giggled
loudly.

A little while later, the two of them practiced their flying!

Just as the two new friends started having fun, Woodstock's friends appeared.

They wanted Woodstock
to fly with them again.

Woodstock looked from Snoopy to his friends and back again. He decided to leave and join his old friends.

Woodstock sighed sadly as he flew away. But flying wasn't as much fun without the Flying Ace!

Snoopy was sad without his
new friend too.

Then Snoopy heard a noise.
It was Woodstock!
Snoopy was so happy
to see his friend.

And that is the story of how Snoopy and Woodstock met and became best friends!